Journey into the Unknown
The Story of Saint Brendan

This story was adapted by author Ann Carroll
and illustrated by Derry Dillon

IRELAND'S BEST KNOWN STORIES
IN A
NUTSHELL

Published 2015
Poolbeg Press Ltd

123 Grange Hill, Baldoyle
Dublin 13, Ireland

Text © Poolbeg Press Ltd 2015

A catalogue record for this book is available from the British Library.

ISBN 978 1 78199 925 7

Cover design and illustrations by Derry Dillon
Printed by GPS Colour Graphics Ltd, Alexander Road, Belfast BT6 9HP

This book belongs to

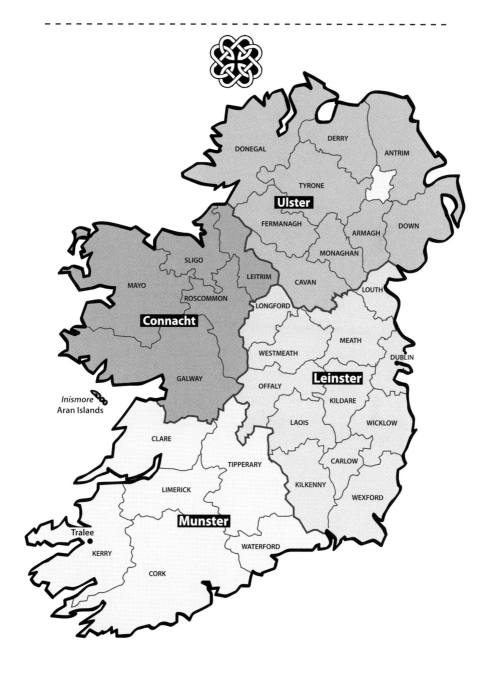

Also in the Nutshell series

A Special Baby

"Our child will be a boy," Cara told her husband Finnlug. "And his future is bright, for I dreamed of angels welcoming his birth with beautiful songs."

And, a few days later, in the year 484 AD, at a small village near Tralee in County Kerry, Cara's baby boy was born.

"A child with such a bright future must be baptised by an important person," his father decided.

1

So they took the baby to Saint Erc, the local bishop.

"We'll call him Brendan," said Erc. "It's a good strong name for a special baby."

Brendan's Childhood and Youth

Bishop Erc watched over the child as he grew up and made sure he was well educated and a good Christian.

The boy took a great interest in the lives of monks and their monasteries. He also loved the sea and became an excellent sailor.

When his schooldays were over, Brendan told Bishop Erc, "If possible, I wish to visit monks living on remote islands and headlands and learn from their way of life."

Erc gave his permission and ordained him as a priest.

Early Travels

Brendan set off, sailing to many lonely places around Ireland. He also visited Iona in Scotland and voyaged to Wales, and even as far as Brittany in France.

The monks he met were very different from each other. Some were teachers. Many worked hard in the fields. Others were great artists creating wonderful illustrated manuscripts. And the hermits, who lived alone, generally spent their time praying.

'We don't all have to be the same, or do the same things to live a good life,' Brendan thought.

The Island of the Blessed

One day Brendan heard a voice telling him to make a journey to the Island of the Blessed, across the sea to the west.

"There you will find the Perfect Place," the voice told him, "where everyone is happy."

Brendan knew such a journey needed careful preparation. So he set about building a boat made of greased leather skins over a wooden frame, and finished it off with the best sail he could make.

Then he chose fourteen companions: good-tempered, strong, reliable monks.

They sailed to Inismore, one of the Aran Islands, to seek the blessing of Saint Enda.

Returning to Kerry, they fasted and prayed for forty days and loaded the boat, which was moored on a little creek, with enough food for six weeks.

At last they were ready.

The Latecomers

Just as they were about to set off, three monks rushed down to the creek and clambered on board.

"What do you think you're doing?" Brendan shouted.

"We heard you're going to a Perfect Place and we want to come too!" said one.

"We want adventure!" said the second.

"You should have picked us and we're not getting off!" cried the third.

"Right!" Brendan snapped. "Be it on your own heads. You've done no preparation and no good will come to you. Don't say you haven't been warned."

And so they set sail on a voyage that would take seven years.

The Empty Island

After forty days the wind dropped and, surrounded by an endless sea, they were beginning to feel low and fearful.

They prayed mightily and suddenly Brendan shouted, "Look! Over there!"

A green and pleasant island appeared in the distance. By rowing vigorously they reached it before sundown.

The monks walked the paved streets and viewed the beautiful buildings with some amazement, for there was no one around, not a solitary person. Only a dog.

The dog led them to a glorious palace whose golden doors were open. Inside they found food and drink, gold and silver treasures, and in the bedrooms there were beautiful paintings.

Brendan told them, "We'll eat, drink, rest and take some food with us tomorrow. Whoever has left all this is very trusting and so we will take only what we need."

The Fate of the First Latecomer

As they were heading to the shore next morning, Brendan noticed that the first latecomer was staggering.

"What's up with you?" he asked. "You look weighed down! What's in your pocket?"

The monk looked guilty and said, "I took a silver necklet. And it's getting heavier by the second! I can hardly carry it."

Before he could utter another word he was struck dead in punishment for robbing the treasure.

Brendan addressed his crew. "Well, he wasn't invited and this is his fate. I warned him!"

And the other two latecomers climbed on board a lot less jauntily than on the first day.

The Paradise of Birds

After some time they reached an island covered with birds.

Here they celebrated Easter. The birds sang beautifully and in their songs Brendan heard descriptions of the places the monks would visit.

The monks thought Easter had never been so wonderful.

As they set sail again the birds followed them out to sea, singing all the while.

And long after the flock had turned back to land, the glory of their voices lingered in the memory.

The Strangest Island Yet

One day the crew saw a strange sight and, as they approached, the conversation went like this:

"Do you think it's an island?"

"Well, it's big enough!"

"But it's all smooth and black."

"There's not a tree or a flower on it!"

When they reached it, a few of the monks jumped on, and set a fire in order to cook some meat in a cauldron. Soon the fire began to blaze.

Suddenly the island heaved and water spouted into the sky.

In a panic the monks got back on board and they sailed away in haste just before the island disappeared under the sea, taking the cauldron with it.

When they were some miles away, Brendan turned to his crew. "That wasn't an island at all! It was an enormous whale!"

The monks were flabbergasted.

Finally one said, "Then we had a lucky escape. He couldn't have been too happy with a fire on his back!"

The Ice Island

By now they'd been a long time away and were
very tired.

So one night, when the waters were calm and
the night starry and bright, the voyagers were
glad to sleep soundly and let the boat drift on.

But at daylight they woke, shivering, to bitter
weather.

Looming up beside them were jagged cliffs of ice. The silence was eerie, broken only by the creaking shifting sound of the ice walls.

The monks' hands froze to the oars. Nonetheless they rowed for hours until the huge iceberg was behind them and warmer air defrosted their hands.

Monsters!

Sighing with relief, they were just relaxing when a great snake-like creature reared out of the sea in front of them, mouth gaping, ready to swallow the boat.

"Oh dear God!" the monks groaned and began to pray.

Then a second monster, breathing fire, rose from the deep to a height of twenty metres.

The prayers turned to a terrified wail. "We'll be burned alive or eaten alive!"

But the second monster breathed his fire on the first and after a mighty battle the Fire-Breather won and the Great Snake was dead, floating on the water in three pieces.

The monks hauled in one of the pieces for food and, when they turned to thank the Fire-Breather, he was gone.

The Fate of the Second Latecomer

Some years into their voyage they stayed on the
Island of Three Choirs, so called because each
person on the island had a marvellous singing
voice and belonged to one of the choirs.

Their melodies lifted the monks' hearts; the sound was angelic.

When they were leaving, the second late-comer said, "I'm going to stay in this pleasant place."

"No, you're not!" Brendan told him. "You're not invited, so just get on the boat!"

Unwillingly the monk went to step on board, missed his footing and disappeared under the sea.

"I warned him at the beginning," Brendan said. "But he took no notice!"

The third latecomer began to feel very afraid.

Danger!

The gryphon swooped on the boat from the sky. It was a huge creature with the head and wings of an eagle and the body of a lion.

The monks were frantic, trying to beat it away with their oars. The gryphon's long talons clawed at their flesh and left them bleeding. The monks knew they would soon tire and be ripped apart by this vile monster.

Then from above came a large bird. Bomb-diving, he pierced the gryphon's breast with his sword-like beak so that the strange beast was fatally wounded and dropped dead into the sea. Their rescuer flew off while the monks clapped and shouted in praise.

The Third Latecomer

The next island they came to was horrible.

The mountains were burning, the rivers were on fire, giants hurled blazing rocks and hot ash at the unfortunate travellers.

"We won't stop here!" Brendan decided, but the third latecomer had already jumped from the boat onto the hot land.

At once he was surrounded by demons and led away, weeping and wailing. Soon he disappeared into the flames.

"He should have listened to me," Brendan sighed. "I warned him that first day!"

The Saddest Island in the World

On a grey rainy day the voyagers sailed up to a
tiny island, more like a large rock.

Brendan spied someone sitting on it. "Who
are you?" he called.

"I'm Judas," a miserable-looking man replied.

"I must stay here as punishment for betraying Christ. Every night I'm tormented by demons."

He wept and Brendan pitied him. "We'll fight your demons for one night, so you may rest. Then we must sail on."

Judas slept peacefully the whole night while the monks kept him safe with their prayers.

Next morning they sailed away to their last island.

Island of the Blessed

At last Brendan and his monks reached the Promised Land, the Island of the Blessed.

Here no one ever got sick, grew old or died. Everyone was happy. No one caused pain or suffered.

This, Brendan realised, was the Perfect Place he had been told to find.

Brendan thought that, now the long voyage was over, this was where they would stay.

"No, you must return home," a young man told him.

"Why? When we went through so much to get here?"

"Because you must tell others your story, so they know it's not easy to get here, but yet it's worth all the trouble."

Brendan nodded. "Like the journey through life," he said.

Home

So Brendan and his original crew of fourteen monks sailed back to Ireland and spent the rest of their lives telling of the wonders they'd seen during their seven-year voyage.

It's said Brendan lived out his final days at a monastery he founded in Clonfert on the River Shannon. People came from all over to hear his stories.

Fact or Fantasy?

As the centuries passed, however, people began to believe that Brendan's voyage never happened, that it was all a fantasy.

But gradually opinion changed again and now many believe Brendan crossed the Atlantic and actually reached Newfoundland in America and that this was, in fact, the Island of the Blessed – a place so far away it was another world.

If true, then Brendan reached America about 500 years before the Vikings and nearly 1000 years before Christopher Columbus!

In 1976, the explorer Tim Severin proved such a voyage was possible when he built a boat just like Brendan's and sailed across the Atlantic to Newfoundland.

Brendan died in 577 AD, famous forever and everywhere as Brendan the Great Navigator and Adventurer.

The End

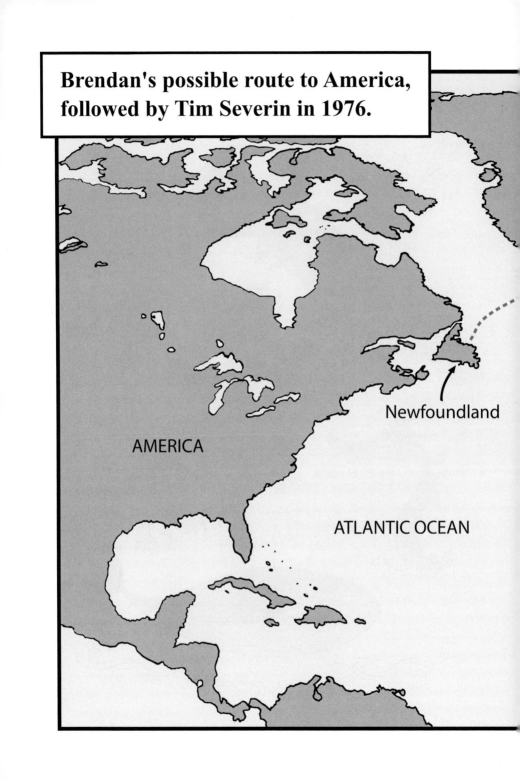

Brendan's possible route to America, followed by Tim Severin in 1976.

AMERICA

Newfoundland

ATLANTIC OCEAN

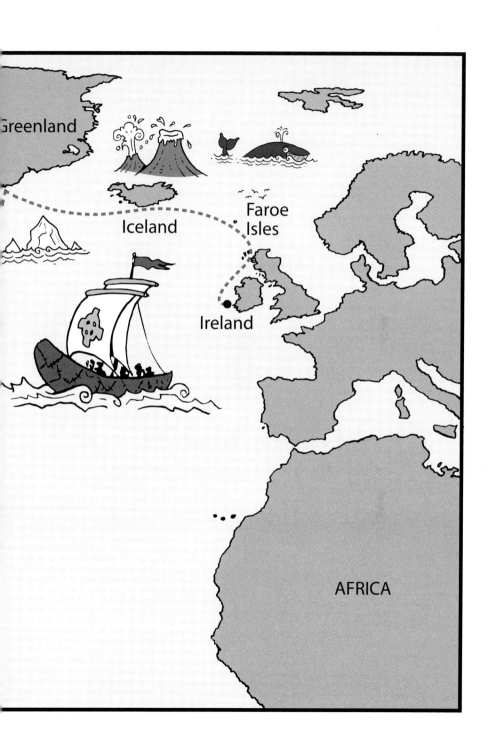

If you enjoyed this book from
Poolbeg why not visit our website:

www.poolbeg.com

and get another book delivered straight
to your home or to a friend's home.

All books despatched within 24 hours.

POOLBEG

Why not join our mailing list
at www.poolbeg.com and get some
fantastic offers, competitions,
author interviews and much more?

@PoolbegBooks